Hello, Family Members,

Learning to read is one of the most [...]ments of early childhood. **Hello Reade**[...] [...]ks are designed to help children become skilled readers who like to read. Beginning readers learn to read by remembering frequently used words like "the," "is," and "and"; by using phonics skills to decode new words; and by interpreting picture and text clues. These books provide both the stories children enjoy and the structure they need to read fluently and independently. Here are suggestions for helping your child *before*, *during*, and *after* reading:

Before

• Look at the cover and pictures and have your child predict what the story is about.
• Read the story to your child.
• Encourage your child to chime in with familiar words and phrases.
• Echo read with your child by reading a line first and having your child read it after you do.

During

• Have your child think about a word he or she does not recognize right away. Provide hints such as "Let's see if we know the sounds" and "Have we read other words like this one?"
• Encourage your child to use phonics skills to sound out new words.
• Provide the word for your child when more assistance is needed so that he or she does not struggle and the experience of reading with you is a positive one.
• Encourage your child to have fun by reading with a lot of expression . . . like an actor!

After

• Have your child keep lists of interesting and favorite words.
• Encourage your child to read the books over and over again. Have him or her read to brothers, sisters, grandparents, and even teddy bears. Repeated readings develop confidence in young readers.
• Talk about the stories. Ask and answer questions. Share ideas about the funniest and most interesting characters and events in the stories.

I do hope that you and your child enjoy this book.

—Francie Alexander
Reading Specialist,
Scholastic's Learning Ventures

To Airplane Derek
— L.J.H.

For Northcountry lightning
watchers Shane, Autumn,
Brittaney, and Cherryne Geidel
— J.W.

Text copyright © 1999 by Lorraine Jean Hopping.
Illustrations copyright © 1999 by Jody Wheeler.
All rights reserved. Published by Scholastic Inc.
SCHOLASTIC, HELLO READER! and CARTWHEEL BOOKS and associated
logos are trademarks and/or registered trademarks of Scholastic Inc.

Library of Congress Cataloging-In-Publication Data

Hopping, Lorraine Jean.
    Wild weather: lightning! / by Lorraine Jean Hopping ; illustrated by Jody Wheeler.
        p. cm. — (Hello reader! Science. Level 4)
    Summary: Describes the power of lightning and its positive and negative effects on living things. Includes safety tips on what to do in case lightning strikes.
    ISBN 0-590-52285-X
    1. Lightning — Juvenile literature. [1. Lightning. 2. Safety.]
I. Wheeler, Jody, ill. II. Title. III. Series.
QC966.5.H66 1999
551.56'32—dc21   98-7656
                                                                            CIP
                                                                            AC

10 9 8 7   02 03 04
                            Printed in the U.S.A.   24
                          First printing, March 1999

⚡ WILD WEATHER ⚡

Lightning!

by Lorraine Jean Hopping
Illustrated by Jody Wheeler

Hello Reader! Science — Level 4

SCHOLASTIC INC.
New York   Toronto   London   Auckland   Sydney

Chapter 1

Bolts From the Blue

Fear of lightning is nothing new.
Meet Zeus, a mighty god of
ancient Greece.
When Zeus got angry,
he threw thunderbolts—
lightning—at people.
But Zeus's anger is just a myth,
an old story.

Real lightning is scarier than
that.
It is most dangerous at the start
of a storm.

An easy breeze may be blowing.
The sky may even be blue.
Then crack!

Out of the sky comes a bolt—
a surprise lightning strike.

Sherri Spain, a teacher from
Memphis, Tennessee,
once loved thunderstorms.
On August 27, 1989, she went
outside to watch a storm brew.
Sherri even brought a snack—
a bag of corn chips.
She leaned against a steel door.
In an instant, her bag exploded.
Lightning knocked Sherri off
her feet!
The lightning hit the steel door
and jumped onto her.

Sherri lost some sight and hearing.
The color drained from her dark
brown hair, turning it white.
Perhaps worst of all, Sherri lost
some of her memory.

In front of her class, she couldn't remember history facts. She even forgot her students' names. By studying hard every day, Sherri retrained her brain. But a single lightning bolt changed her life forever.

Sherri's lightning strike was an accident.
But scientist Maribeth Stolzenburg risks "Zeus's fury" on purpose.
She studies lightning outdoors.
Maribeth knows that Zeus isn't really the cause of lightning bolts.
Electricity is.
Lightning bolts are powerful electric sparks in the sky.

Maribeth and six other scientists launch weather balloons into the middle of thunderstorms.
Thunderstorms are storms that make lightning.

In the summer, South Baldy Mountain in central New Mexico is a thunderstorm factory.
Each afternoon, dark clouds roll over the mountain.

As the storm forms, Maribeth and her team set up weather balloons. The balloons need space to lift off. Trees and power lines would get in the way.
Unfortunately, lightning strikes the highest points.
And in open space, the scientists are the tallest targets around. The team works fast to avoid being a bull's-eye for "Zeus."

The balloon is inside a yellow, tube-shaped bag the size of a small car.
It is already blown up.
The scientists rip off a long strip to open the tube.
Then they run for cover.

The white balloon is filled with
helium, a gas lighter than air.
It soars up into the storm.
It is as thin as a party balloon,
but tougher.

For twenty minutes or so,
the balloon rises through
wind, rain, and hail.
Then it bursts and parachutes
back to Earth.

One instrument on the balloon measures the electricity in the storm.
Another measures rain and hail (bits of ice).
Radio signals send the data to a computer.

Safe inside a nearby building, Maribeth watches the data appear on a computer image of the storm. She looks for surprises.

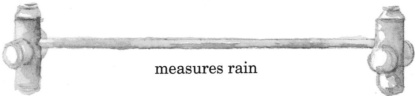

measures rain

sends radio signals to ground

measures electricity

For example, one balloon found
more charges than expected in
the storm's anvil.
The anvil is a cloud that juts out
from the rest of the storm.
Now, Maribeth's challenge is
to find out why.

anvil

"I'm studying the same thing that Benjamin Franklin studied two hundred years ago," Maribeth says.

In 1752, Franklin did history's most famous lightning experiment.
He flew a kite with a metal key attached to it.
The key attracted lightning.
Franklin proved that lightning is not fire, as people thought.
It is electricity.
His lightning experiments were far more dangerous than Maribeth's.
One scientist died trying to copy them.

"We still don't know much about what causes lightning," says Maribeth. "But the more you know, the scarier it is."

How and why does electricity move around in a storm?
What makes lightning zig and zag?
Can we predict where it will strike?
All of these questions are, in a sense, still up in the air.

Chapter 2

Hot Spots

Say "lightning strike" aloud. That takes about a second. Every second of every day, lightning strikes Earth an average of one hundred times. Right now, nearly two thousand storms are pounding our planet. By midnight tonight, today's storm total could top forty thousand!

Thunderstorms form everywhere except the cold, dry polar regions.

Most storms break out in Earth's
hot spots, places near the equator.
The air is warmer and wetter
there.
Heat is the "fuel" of
thunderstorms.

The Average Number of Thunderstorm Days in a Year

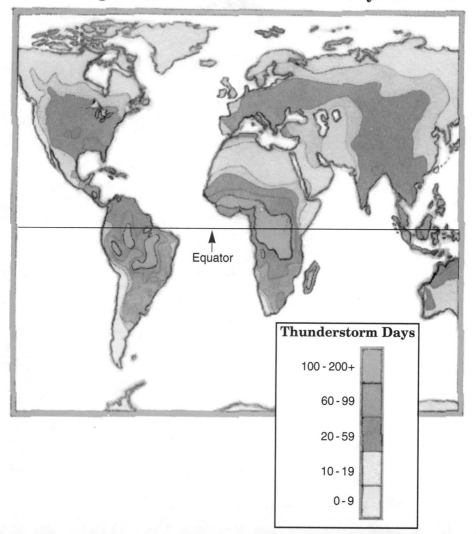

Equator

Thunderstorm Days

100 - 200+

60 - 99

20 - 59

10 - 19

0 - 9

Warm, wet Florida is the top lightning "hot spot" of North America — by far.

Lightning hits several hundred Americans each year.
Like teacher Sherri Spain, seven out of ten victims survive.

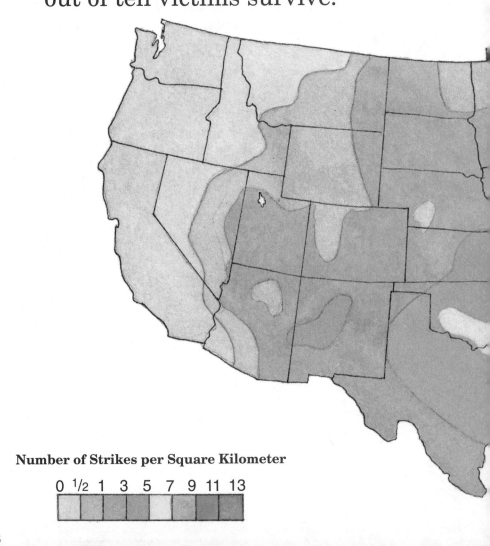

Number of Strikes per Square Kilometer

0 ½ 1 3 5 7 9 11 13

Lightning is very powerful.
But it flashes in and out of a body
faster than you can blink.
It often doesn't have time to kill.

The chances of being hit are one
in a million for most Americans.
People who work and play outside
are more at risk.

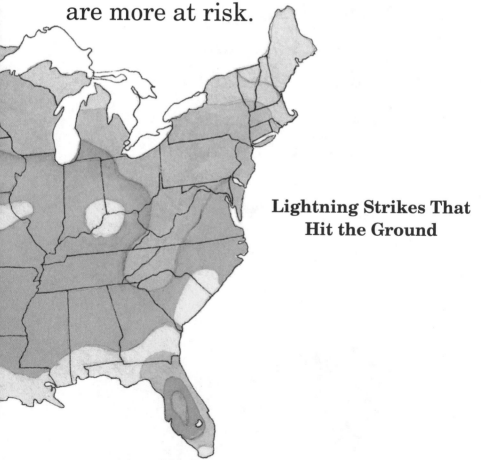

**Lightning Strikes That
Hit the Ground**

Source: Richard E. Orville, Texas A & M University; 1991

In 1992, Toy Trice was practicing with his high school football team in Burtonsville, Maryland.
A bolt tore through his helmet.
It burned his jersey and blasted his football cleats right off his feet!

The electric shock stopped Toy's heart from beating.
Luckily, someone knew CPR, a first aid treatment to restart the heart.
Toy escaped with minor injuries.

Roy Sullivan, a former park ranger,
has been hit seven times.
He lost his hair, his eyebrows,
and a toenail.
But he survived all seven strikes.

The Empire State Building
in New York City has been hit
more than a thousand times.
A metal pole called a lightning
rod attracts lightning.
Then it channels the
electricity
safely to the
ground.

Jets get hit often — about once
or twice a year per airplane.
The electricity travels through
the metal body of the plane, so it
doesn't harm the people inside.

In February 1998, a bolt struck a
jet in Birmingham, Alabama.
It knocked out the landing gear.
The pilot landed the jet on its
nose and belly, tearing
a hole in the aircraft.
The plane stopped in
a muddy field.
Everyone jumped
off safely.

A direct lightning hit is very serious. In August 1991, Gretel Ehrlich was hiking in the Wyoming wilderness. The next thing she knew, she woke up on the ground, stunned. "The lightning bolt made me arch back like a fish in a frying pan," Gretel later wrote in a book.

Gretel's legs went limp.
She couldn't see or talk.
Her skin had feathery burns called "Lichtenberg's flowers."
The electricity had followed the moisture in and on her body.
It flowed through the sweat and rain on her skin.
It traveled by way of her blood vessels.
Gretel dragged herself to safety as the storm raged around her.

Lightning doesn't have to strike directly to do damage.
The electric charge can travel along the ground.
Cows or sheep in a field can die from a nearby strike.

People standing under a tree
are even less safe.
A bolt can strike the tree,
sending a charge in all directions.
People closest to the tree feel the
most powerful shock.

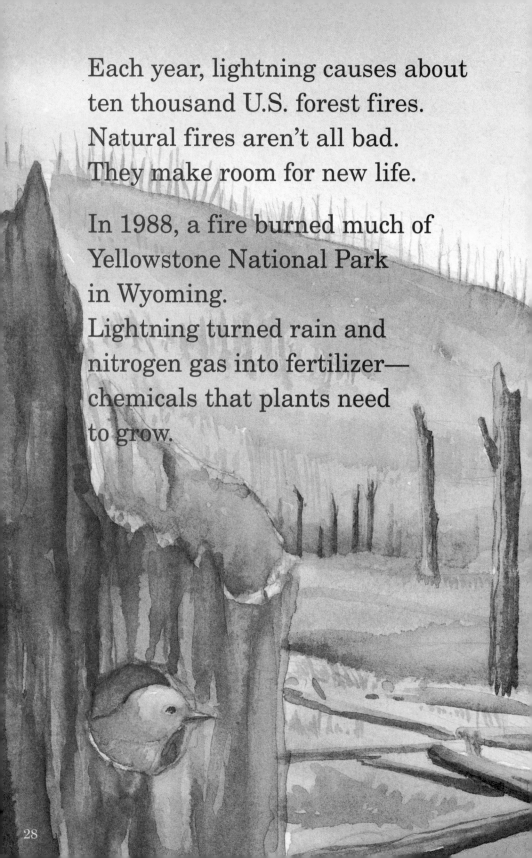

Each year, lightning causes about
ten thousand U.S. forest fires.
Natural fires aren't all bad.
They make room for new life.

In 1988, a fire burned much of
Yellowstone National Park
in Wyoming.
Lightning turned rain and
nitrogen gas into fertilizer—
chemicals that plants need
to grow.

The heat of the fire opened up pine cones, freeing the seeds inside.

The seeds quickly grew into trees. Beetles moved in to chew up the dead, burned wood.

Woodpeckers arrived to eat the beetles.

Bluebirds built nests in the holes left by the woodpeckers.

Chapter 3

An Electric Sandwich

Thunderstorms are the main
makers of lightning, but not the
only makers.
Snowstorms, sandstorms, and
even volcanoes can create
lightning.

What do these lightning makers
have in common?
Billions of bits floating in the air:
ice, sand, dust, ash, or chemicals.
Air currents cause the bits to
swirl and crash together.
Crashing bits create friction,
or rubbing.

Rub your hands together really fast.
Feel the warmth?
Friction creates heat.
It also creates electricity.
On a dry day, pet a fluffy cat.
Then touch something metal.
You may feel and hear a spark.
This spark is just like lightning,
only much smaller.

Friction creates two types of
charges: positive and negative.
For unknown reasons, the charges
in a storm cloud form layers, like
an electric sandwich.
The top of the clouds and the
ground have positive charges.
Negative charges form the "meat"
in the middle.

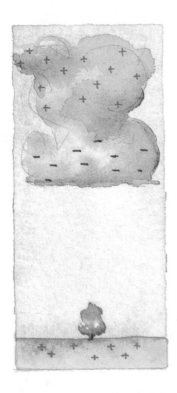

Opposites attract.
Negative and positive charges try
to jump toward each other.
But the air acts like a wall.
Soon, the charges are too strong
for the air to stop them.
They zap together, sparking a
stroke of lightning.
Many strokes may follow the same
path, creating flickers of light.

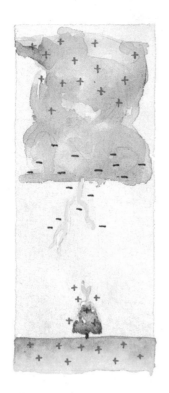

A lightning stroke may go from one part of a cloud to another part.
It may jump from one cloud to another cloud.
But the scariest lightning strikes between a cloud and the ground.

The stroke may be many miles long.
It can shine brighter than ten million light bulbs.
It may be five times hotter than the surface of the sun.

The heat causes gases in the air to expand rapidly.
The expanding gases vibrate or shake.
The vibrating air creates a shock of sound called thunder.

If you see a flash but don't hear thunder, the lightning is more than 15 miles (24 kilometers) away. The sound dies before reaching you or passes way over your head.

Light travels faster than sound. So you usually see a flash first. Then you "hear" seconds of silence. The more seconds, the farther the lightning is from you.

Sound from the closest part of the lightning arrives first. The thunder growls on and on. At last, the farthest sounds arrive and the thunder dies out.

Maribeth Stolzenburg once saw a flash and heard a boom at the same time. The lightning was only about two football fields away!

Sound from this part of
lightning travels farther.
It takes longer to reach you.

Sound from
this part
reaches you
first.

Chapter 4

Jets, Sprites, and Elves

For fun, Maribeth likes to
keep an eye on lightning.
From a safe spot, she watches for
a flash.
Then she closes her eyes right
away.
The pattern of the lightning shines
on her eyelids, just for a moment.
"It's like a camera flash," she says.
The flashes are like snowflakes.
Each one looks different.

Ribbon lightning is one of many
lightning types.
It begins with a flash.
Then the wind pushes the
lightning's path a little.
A second bolt strikes near the first
one, and perhaps another bolt.
Each bolt is as thin as your thumb.
But together, they look like a fat
ribbon of light.

Ball lightning is a rare, glowing globe of electricity the size of a baseball or basketball.
It may be gold, blue, white, green, or red.

In 1980, Mount St. Helens volcano in Washington created ball lightning.
The glowing orbs tumbled on the ground like ping-pong balls.

St. Elmo's fire is not really a fire.
It's a blue glow of electricity.
It appears on the tips of objects—
the masts of a ship, the horns of
a steer.

Jets are fountains of blue light.
Sprites are red, glowing balls.
Elves are green bursts of
electricity.

All three forms of lightning appear
high above the storm clouds.
Pilots sometimes see them.
But they flash very, very fast.
And they are very dim.
People knew almost nothing about
jets, sprites, and elves until the
1990s.
Scientists are still learning how
and why they happen.

Chapter 5

Lightning in a Lab

Scientists can "make lightning." That is, they can trigger a bolt during a storm.

They launch small rockets attached to a very long, thin wire. The wire provides a path for electricity to follow.

Scientists study step-by-step pictures of the triggered strikes. One goal is to help power companies avoid lightning strikes.

Lightning can wipe out a city's power in a flash.

Indoors, scientists can create
"lightning" in a laboratory.
A machine called a Van de Graaff
generator makes electric charges.
The charges leap to a metal pole.
Instant lightning!

The metal "bird cage" looks like
a scary place to be.
On the outside, it has enough
electricity to kill a human.
But inside the cage, it is
perfectly safe.

In a way, North America is one big lightning laboratory. A Lightning Detection Network is spread around the continent. These sensors detect lightning. Within seconds, they report the strikes to a central computer. The strikes appear as dots on a computer map.

Lightning Strikes During One Storm

Chicago, IL

+ = lightning strike   Source: Global Atmospherics, Inc.

Scientists study the map and other data to forecast the day's weather. A storm warning means that lightning is near.

Amusement park rides shut down, because metal machines invite lightning.

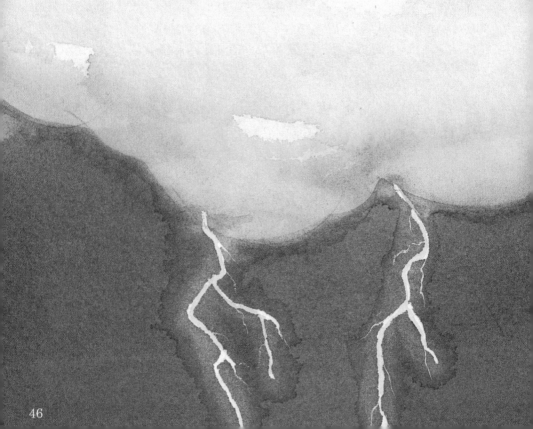

Lifeguards order everybody out of the swimming pool, because electricity flows well through water.

Reporters warn people to take cover.
Anyone who wants to escape "Zeus's fury" listens.

Lightning Safety Tips

What should you do when you see or hear lightning? Take cover!

- If you are on a telephone, hang up.
- If you are outside, go inside a big building.
- If no building is around, stay in a car. Roll up all windows.
- If no car is around, find a low area. But don't hide in a ditch. It might flood.
- Don't lie down. Instead, crouch into a ball.
- Stay away from water—ponds, rivers, and bathtubs.
- Don't touch metal, such as golf clubs, fishing poles, or canoes.
- Don't stand near tall objects such as trees and poles.